T0145175

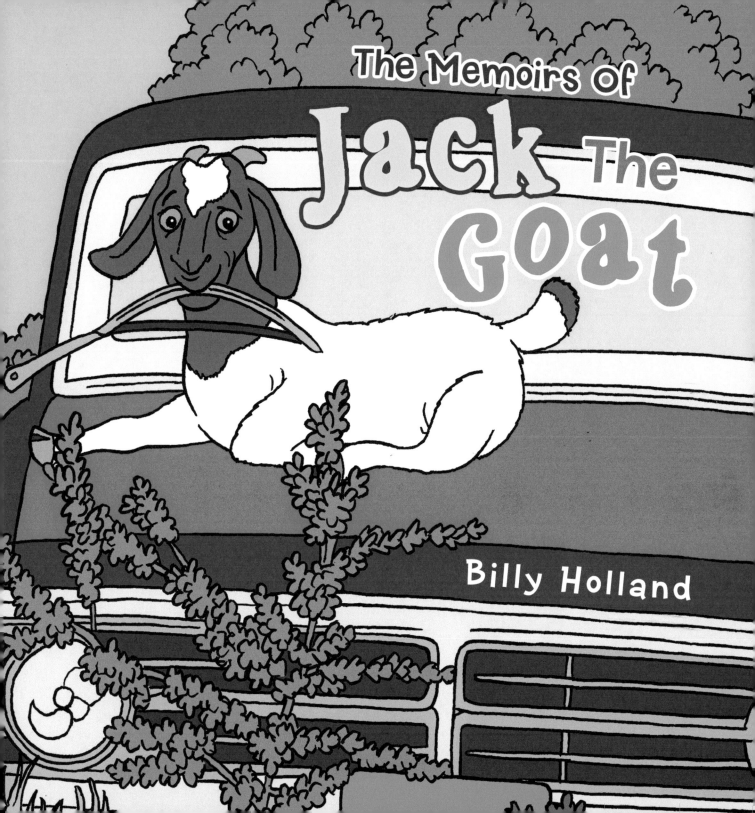

AuthorHouse™
1663 Liberty Drive
Bloomington, IN 47403
www.authorhouse.com
Phone: 833-262-8899

Because of the dynamic nature of the Internet, any web addresses or links contained
in this book may have changed since publication and may no longer be valid. The views
expressed in this work are solely those of the author and do not necessarily reflect the
views of the publisher, and the publisher hereby disclaims any responsibility for them.

Any people depicted in stock imagery provided by Getty Images are models,
and such images are being used for illustrative purposes only.
Certain stock imagery © Getty Images.

This book is printed on acid-free paper.

ISBN: 978-1-6655-6019-1 (sc)
ISBN: 978-1-6655-6020-7 (hc)
ISBN: 978-1-6655-6018-4 (e)

Library of Congress Control Number: 2022909376

Print information available on the last page.

Published by AuthorHouse 05/16/2022

authorHOUSE

Table of Contents

CHAPTER 1
The Sanitation Department

Hi there, my name is Jack, what's yours? My friends call me "General", and my enemies call me "Sir!"

I am an African Boar goat, not one of them scrawny ugly Spanish goats. Us Boar goats are bigger, stronger, and handsomer, than those ole Spanish goats. I got a beautiful brown neck and head, with a white body. My shoulders are broad. My hips are narrow, and I'm ready for trouble, if you know what I mean.

Rachel, my keeper, asked me to put down my MEMOIRS, since I've led such an interesting life. I say that Rachel's my keeper, and I guess that's so Rachel and Ralph, (she calls him uncle) whatever that means, comes to the ranch, to give me fresh water, and some grain to eat. The truth is that I'm more of her keeper, because I do so much around this ranch. I'm head of the Sanitation Department. It's my job to see that things are kept clean and safe for the environment. It's a big job, but somebody has to do it.

This ranch is a big beautiful place, for a goat. It's got lots of rolling hills, with more dry riverbeds than you can shake a stick at. There are lots of crevices to investigate, and just a few trees to get in the way There's lots of Mustard plants, and Sun Flower plants. Oh yeah, there's also an occasional Yucca Cactus. Boy, I hate those Yucca Cactus. One time I accidentally sat on a Yucca! Ouch!... Well, that's another story for another day. It takes a body a good day to cover the whole ranch, with lookin' in and out of every crevice for sanitary stuff, and keepin' the environment clean.

Every day, me and Gomez, (he's my sidekick) we stay busy. He's one of them Spanish goats, and my underling. He takes orders from me. Anyhow, everyday, me and Gomez patrol the crevices and nooks on the ranch, lookin' for anything sanitary. Sometimes Ralph and Rachel put things in one of the crevices, like tree limbs and broken up sidewalks. The leaves on the tree are sanitary, but the rest of those branches are, "uck", too hard and dry, strictly unsanitary! Those rocks were unsanitary, too. I nearly broke a tooth on 'em.

Sometimes they will bring sanitary stuff like old shirts or boots. One time Ralph brought an old rocking chair, with a wicker seat, yummy! That wicker bottom sure was tasty, and those leather strings wrapped around it, were sure good, too. I had to fight off Gomez! He really wanted some of that wicker seat, but since I'm head of the Sanitation Department,

I get the very best, you know what I mean. "General Sir, can I have some of that wicker seat?" Gomez inquired. "Nope." "Well why not? I done helped you find it, Sir" " Sure you helped me find it, but think of your stomach, Private. This here wicker is high class hooch. Your stomach ain't used to such." Your stomach is used to Grama and Johnson grass, and such. Why this here wicker would tear up your stomach, think boy." "You're right General, but what about them leather strings?" "Don't go there Private. Them strings is the same as the wicker, they will tear up your stomach." Gomez bought it. It's like I always say, them Spanish goats is all dumb. Well, that's our job, walking up and down every crevice, lookin' for sanitary stuff, but mostly we have to settle for Grama, and Johnson grass.

At the end of the day, there's nothin' better than to return to the barn. Our side of the barn is shady most of the day, because Ralph built an awning. Rachel put down some fresh hay for me and Gomez to sleep on and there's a big water trough near us. Nothin' better after a hard day's work, than a cool drink and a long nap, know what I mean?

The pigpen is only fifty feet from the barn. When the wind blows from the south, wow, look out, your nostrils is about to be assaulted by the worst odor you can imagine. Gomez likes to hang out at the pigpen. He must have a stuffed up nose, or something, because the odor doesn't seem to bother him. He sticks his head through the slats in the fence that surrounds the pigpen. Just inside the pigpen, is a feed trough. Gomez just loves pig food. One problem though, sometimes he gets his head stuck in the fence. I'll never forget the first time it happened. I was nappin' when Gomez called me. General, I needs some help." I didn't hear him at first, so he shouted: 'GENERAL, I NEEDS SOME HELP!" "What?" I asked groggily. "General, I needs some help. I stuck in the pigpen." So I got up and went over to see what the problem was. There he was, with his head stuck in the fence. When he tried to pull his head out, his horns caught on the slats. "You have to turn your head to get out, Private." I instructed. About that time, Rachel arrived to feed and water us. She saw Gomez with his head stuck in the fence, and felt sorry for him. She tried to get his head out, but could not. Ralph tried, too. He worked with Gomez for over fifteen minutes, but couldn't get the critter loose. Gomez stayed stuck all night. Early the next morning, he finally followed my advice and turned his head just right, and got his head out of the fence. You'd think that he would have learned his lesson, but not that stupid goat. I've lost count of how many times he's gotten his head stuck in the pigpen fence. Some goats just never learn, know what I mean?

Billy lives on the other side of the barn. He's big, but at least he's stupid. He's what they call a mule, but he looks more like a broken down bag of bones, if you ask me. His body is dark brown, his nose is white, and he has three white feet. Rachel rides him round the pasture some, and Ralph uses him to gather stray cattle.

The view from Billy's pen is kinda limited. The only trees on the ranch, block his view on one side. Our barn blocks the view on the other side. The pigpen blocks the view on the other side, so Billy spends a lot of his time looking over the fence on the only side that his view ain't blocked.

Sometimes he puts his head over the fence, turns towards us, and opens his big dumb mouth. He's always asking dumb questions. One time he asked me if I'd seen other mules on the ranch. "Why would I look for any dad blamed mules?" I answered. "Dunno." Billy replied. "Just thought that there might be another mule on this big ranch." "Well, I ain't seen any. I'm too busy doin' sanitation stuff to look for other mules, know what I mean?"

Billy continued.

If you see any mules, will you teil them about me please?" "Sure, Billy, anything to keep you happy." "Is the grass the same color in the pasture, as it is here at the barn?" he asked. "Yeah, it's exactly the same" I answered. "Is there any water to drink in the pasture?" Billy continued. "Sure'nough, there's two ponds where a feller can wet his whistle. One of 'em is kinda small and dries up in the simmer." "Are there any scary animals in the pasture?" Billy asked. "Just coyotes, and they're mean and ugly varmints." "How......?" " That's'nough questions, Billy. I got to get some sleep, know what I mean?"

Billy would've talked all night. I guess he gets kinda lonely staying by his self all day. But a feller gotta get his rest. The sanitation business is hard work. I got a long drink from the water trough, turned around three times on a pile of hay, and lay myself down. I was sawing logs in no time...........

Next morning dawned early. I got up and stretched myself good. Then I kicked Gomez. "Private, rise and shine," I ordered, "Get them peepers open." "What?" Gomez said with a start. "Get up boy," I said. It's time to get to work." "Sir, I'm up, General," Gomez answered.

We searched the ranch over all morning. Couldn't hardly find nothin' sanitary to eat. Some days is like that. We finally had to settle for some young, tender, Gramma Grass. The sun was high in the sky, and all was well. So me and Gomez began to fill our bellies.

Next thing I knew, my feet was all wet. I looked down to see that I was standing in some black goop. "General, what's that goop you're standing in?" Gomez asked. "Don't rightly know, Private," I answered. "Well, what do it smell like?" Gomez wanted to know. So I took a sniff. "Uck, that goop smell awful." "What do it taste like?" Gomez asked. "Don't know that neither." Gomez lapped up some of the black goop with his tongue. His eyes crossed and he started coughing. He took to runnin' in circles. Then he lit out for the barn and didn't stop till he got there. I stepped out of the goop and tried to wipe it off my hoofs, but it were too sticky to come off. I rolled in the grass, but that didn't help none neither, so I mosied back to the barn, leaving a trail of black goop.

Gomez had his head stuck in the pigpen eating the grain, so that he could get that nasty taste out of his mouth. Billy noticed right off, that I had that black goop on my legs. "What's that black goop on your legs, General?" he asked. "Don't know for sure, Billy", I answered. "Where did it come from?" he inquired. "From the pasture", I responded. I bent over and put my front knees and forehead on the ground, while I pushed myself with my back legs. "What you doin' now, General?" Billy questioned. "Trying to wipe this goop off my legs." "Is it working?" Billy asked. "Not too well." Then I sat on my bottom and pushed backwards with my front feet. "Is that rubbing the goop off?" Billy continued. "Nope, not so much." "What's the Private doin?" Billy wanted to know. "Immm wa sh th goo o my mo.", Gomez answered. "What did he say?"

Billy questioned, "He said that he was a trying to get that black goop out of his mouth," I answered. "How did he get that goop in his mouth in the first place?" Billy inquired. "I ain't got no more time for fool questions. I gotta get this goop offa me, don't you know?", I shouted at Billy.

I started rolling around in the grass, and pushing myself along the ground with my forehead down. I even got down on all four knees, and crawled across the grass, trying to wipe that black goop off.

Directly, Rachel and Ralph showed up to give me some food and water. When she saw the black goop on my feet, she came over to have a closer look. She rubbed her forefinger in the goop, and smelled it. She started hopping up and down, like her pants was on fire. She yelled for Ralph, and he came a running. When he saw the black goop, he took his forefinger and wiped some off my leg. Then he smelled it, and tasted it. Yuck! Quick as a flash, he spit that goop out. He grabbed Rachel's hand and began to do a little dance. He picked her up off the ground, and whirled her around. They were both yellin' and laughin'. It was plumb ridiculous. I's never seen Rachel and Ralph act so silly. Me, Billy, and the Private, just look at them. I had no idea what had gotten into them.

Ralph told Rachel to get Billy's saddle from the barn. He opened the gate to Billy's pen, and brought him out. Quick as a flash, he saddled Billy and put the bit in his mouth. "General, what's goin'on?", Billy asked. "Don't rightly know, Billy," I answered. "But I aims to find out. "Where are they taking me?", Billy wondered. "Don't worry none," I responded. I follow along to find out what's up. By this time, Ralph had Billy saddled, and he and Rachel mounted. Rachel's hair was a blowin' in the wind, and Ralph's belly was a floppin' up and down. They followed the black goop that had dripped off my feet. As they went, Ralph shouted at the top of his lungs: "Jack's discovered oil! Jack's discovered oil?"

"General, what is oil?" Gomez asked. "Don't rightly know, Private, but I aims to find out. Your eyes uncrossed, yet?" "Yes sir," Gomez snapped. I looked into his eyes, and sure 'nough they'd uncrossed. "Ok Private, let's follow 'em and see what's up.

Me and Gomez followed that trail of black goop, that had dropped off my legs. Soon 'nough, we found Billy, Ralph, and Rachel. They were standin' 'round the place where me and Gomez found the black goop. The goop had formed a small pond by now. It was pitch black, and smelled to high heaven.

Ralph and Rachel walked around the small goop pond a couple of times. Ralph found an old dried up Yucca stem, and stuck it into the pond. The black goop covered nearly half of the Yucca stem. Ralph and Rachel talked real loud and real fast. I couldn't make our what they was sayin'.

Me and Gomez got bored watching them walk 'round the little pond and talkin' so fast. We went back to the barn to get a cold drink of water, and a nice nap. Later on, Ralph, Rachel, and Billy, rode back to the barn. They unsaddled Billy and went to their home. Me? I had another good nap.

CHAPTER 3
The Yellow Monster

The next morning I woke with a start, to this awful racket. There was these two horseless chariots drivin' through the pasture. One of 'em belonged to Ralph, and the other one, I didn't know. Being in charge of the Sanitation Department, I naturally had to investigate.

I slipped off and left Gomez sawin' logs on the hay. I followed the two horseless chariots to the place where I'd gotten into that black goop. Ralph and another feller was lookin' 'round. Ralph talked real loud and waved his hands 'round a lot.

Finally, they got back into their horseless chariots and left. I went back to the barn to catch a few more z's. I'd just gotten back to sleep, and was having a wonderful dream about some sanitary stuff that Ralph had dropped off in the ravine, when this deep growl woke me. It woke Gomez and Billy, too. "General, what's that noise?" Billy asked. "Dunno, but will find out," I answered. "Can I come, too?", Gomez wanted to know. "Sure, come on Private, let's go."

We found this big yellow monster, slowly crawling along the ground. It made enough noise to wake the dead. It belched black smoke, and stirred up lots of dirt and dust. Me and Gomez couldn't get too close, because of all the dirt flying 'round. "What's that monster doing?", Gomez wanted to know. It's eating dirt," I answered. "Why?" "Dunno," I replied. "But let's keep our eyes on it for a while." Me and Gomez watched the yellow monster. All it done, was crawl slowly along the ground, toward the place where I got that black goop on my feet. Then it turned'round, and started moving back toward us.

In due time, another one of them horseless chariots showed up, but this one was much bigger than Ralph's. It pulled a wagon behind it, and in the wagon was another yellow monster, only smaller than the first one. The horseless chariot stopped near that place where I found the black goop. A man got out and climbed on top of the second yellow monster. He drove it off the wagon, and started scooping up dirt with the monster's big mouth. The monster picked up a big mouthful of dirt, carried it to a ravine, and dropped the dirt in there. "Why is that little monster moving that dirt?", Gomez wondered. "Dunno," I responded. Both yellow monsters kept at it all day, movin' over the ground, stirring up the dirt, and the other one, moving dirt from place to place. It got boring after a while, so me and Gomez started lookin' for something sanitary to eat.

Around dark, me and Gomez started back to the barn. On the way, we saw the two monsters. They weren't movin', and lay still and quiet. We just had to investigate, know what I mean?

"What them monsters doing?" Gomez inquired. "They're sleepin'," I answered. "Private, go over there and see if you can wake those monsters." "No sir," Gomez protested. "They might eat me!" "That's an order, Private. Shake those monsters and see if you can wake them." "Why don't you do it, General?" Gomez begged. "Private, you have your orders, now carry them out." "Si."

Gomez walked cautiously over to the monsters. He quickly touched the smallest monster with his front paw. It didn't move or make any noise. He then touched it again with his nose. Nothin'. "Try the other monster," I ordered. Gomez walked cautiously over to the larger monster, and touched it with his nose. Nothin'. He then reared up on his back feet, and put his front feet on the big ugly monster. "They must be asleep," I exclaimed. "Thank goodness," Gomez responded. Since they was asleep, I walked over for a closer look. "Let me see if there's anythin' sanitary on these monsters," I said. Gomez started sniffin' 'round the smaller monster, while I sniffed the larger one. Mostly, the monster smelled like dirt, and that dad blamed black goop. I sure 'nough didn't want to get any of that goop in my mouth, yuck! Part of the monster smelled like Grama grass and Sunflowers, yummy! It's my job to check out everythin' on the ranch, to see if it's sanitary, or not. I bit into it. It tasted ok, but was tough and stringy. I pulled on it, but it was stuck to the monster. I pulled harder, and it got longer. The harder I tugged, the longer it got. I chewed and chewed some more. Finally I just spit it out, unsanitary, know what I mean?

Next I started sniffin' 'round a big, black, round thing. There were four of them on the monster. They were kinda like legs on which the monster moved 'round. Then I decided that I'd better mark my territory, so I hiked my leg, and let 'er rip. Don't want Gomez or them coyotes messing with my stuff. Anyhow, I sniffed 'round some more on that big, black, round thing. Then I decided to bite the dad blame thing.

CHAPTER 4

Fenced Out

Next morning, I was woke up by Ralph talkin' loud to another feller. What a horrible and unkind way to be woke up. All that hollerin' and shoutin' right there in my barn, was right bothersome. The other feller looked mad, and kept pointing his anger my way. Finally, he left, and Ralph shut the gate. I guess he didn't want me patrollin' the ranch. "General, why did Ralph lock that gate?", Gomez wondered. "To keep them big yellow monsters out of here." Billy ventured a guess. "I dunno Private, but I aims to find out." With that, I went over to the gate and began to look for a way out. Ain't no gate been invented, that I couldn't find a way out. I'd crawl under, or jump over, or squeeze through somewhere. The gate was shut tight, all right, but it weren't so tall as to keep a feller' from jumpin' over, know what I mean?

Out in the pasture, I found the two monsters still moving dirt, but there were also two more big chariots. Standing right near those two new big chariots, were several men just a talkin' up a storm. They was buzzin' 'round that black goop. Funny thing though, when I stepped in the black goop, it was just a little spot on the ground, no bigger than my water trough back at the barn. Today, that black goop had grown into a sizeable pool Anyhow, those men started buzzin' 'round that pool of black goop, hollerin' back and forth, and a liftin' some sort of metal contraption off one of them big chariots. They placed the metal contraption on the ground, and then started hookin' up all sorts of stuff to it. Right before my eyes, they built themselves a small dirt monster. The monster began to make all kinds of noise, and dirt started flyin'! It made such a terrible noise, that I had to leave. After all, I had to check out the ranch for sanitary stuff, know what I mean?

Later that day, I went back to where the two big chariots were. They was still a makin' a lot a noise. The thing they put on the ground, not only made a lot of noise, but it was growin'! It was growin' fast.

First thing I noticed, was that tower was still a growin'. It hurt my neck when I looked at the top of it. When we got closer, we found a fence, not a short wooden one like back at the barn, but a tall metal one, and there was no jumpin' over it. Me and Gomez prowled 'round it for a long time. The gates were all tightly shut, and there weren't no way to squeeze through or crawl under. Boy, that ticks me off! Some people just don't appreciate the sanitation work I do. . ...

Some days later, Ralph drove up to our pens in his chariot. He backed up slowly, then stopped near the gate. The Private and I mosied over for a closer look. In the back of his chariot, Ralph had this big gray colored cage. I could tell right away that somethin' was alive inside that cage, because the thing vibrated and jerked about, know what I mean.

Ralph opened the gate to the pens, then let down the gate on his chariot. Then he opened the door to the gray colored cage. He grabbed a hold of whatever was in the cage, and began to pull. Whatever was in the cage didn't want to come out. Ralph had to drag it inch by inch, all the way out of the cage. "Look, General," the Private said excitedly, " I sees Horns." Sure 'nough, Ralph had a hold of a set of horns, and pulled the critter out of the cage. It was a goat. Not a handsome African Bore like me, but one of them lowly Spanish goats. "We don't need no other goats about the place," I said. "The Private and me has got the Sanitation Department under control. Take that critter back where it came from." Ralph half pulled, half carried the goat through the gate, and into the small pen next to the pigs. He finally let the critter go, and I got a good look, for the first time. It weren't a he. I mean, it's a girl! She had long slender legs, and a firm rear end. Her coat was as white as mother's milk, and she had beautiful blue eyes. She was a knockout!

I walked over to the pen where Ralph had put her, so we could get better acquainted, know what I mean. Before I could get there, Ralph cut me off. He grabbed Gomez by the horns and put him in the pen with her. That made me so mad, that I saw red! I wanted to meet this fine young nanny. She needed a mature and worldly tough goat, not that goofo, clumsy, awkward, Gomez. Why was Ralph interferin' with my love life? That ticked me off. "No fair," I shouted.

Ralph gave me some food and water, but I weren't interested. I was in love with that angel in the next pen. After givin' Gomez and the nanny some food and water, Ralph took off in his chariot. "Who's the new goat?", Billy inquired. "Dunno, but I aims to find out," I answered. "Why did Ralph put Gomez in the pen with her?" Billy continued to question. "Not now, Billy," I said. "I've got some courtin' to do." I glided over to the new nanny, and introduced myself. "Hello there beautiful," I sighed. "Most everyone 'round here calls me General, but you can call me Jack. What's your name?" "Blondie," she purred. "How did such a beautiful creature like you, end up way out here in the middle of nowhere?" I asked. " I really don't know," she said. "I was at my home, when my owner came out with your owner, and grabbed me by the horns, and put me in that cage. It was awful. It was cramped, and it smelled horrible," Blondie said with a sniffle. "I'm, sorry that you've had such a hard day, little lady," I lamented.. "But I sure am glad that you're here. Your presence makes this place more tolerable," I crooned. "What's her name, General?" Billy interfered. "Blondie," I reported. "She's had a hard day, so knock off the fifty questions game, know what I mean?" "General," Blondie cooed, "Aren't you going to introduce me to this noble giant?" "Why, yes Ma'am, excuse my manners," I responded. "This here is Billy. Billy, meet Blondie," "Nice to meet you, Billy," Blondie replied. "The pleasure is all mine," Billy said, as he bowed his head below his chest. "Gosh, she called me a noble giant. Where are you from, Blondie?" Billy asked. "Until just a little while ago, I lived on a farm, a short distance from here," Blondie replied. I was just telling the General that my owner and your owner, loaded me in a small, foul smelling cage, and brought me here."

"Do you...?" Just a dad blamed minute, Billy," I interrupted, " I haven't introduced Blondie to all the animals on the ranch. That feller over there, is Private Gomez. He assists me in the Sanitation Department, here on the ranch. I'm head of the Sanitation Department, know what I mean? It's my job to rid the ranch of all sanitary stuff. " "Fascinating," Blondie replied. "Does the Private, speak?" "I'm eatin'." Gomez answered. "Does he always get his head stuck in the fence like that?" Blondie asked. "Pretty much," I answered. "He likes the pig food, but when he sticks his head 'tween the slats to get at it, he forgets how to get his head out." "Moron," Blondie responded. "My thoughts exactly," I agreed. "That's why I'm the General, and he's the Private...Say, let me see if I can get into your pen, and make sure everythin' is ok." "Can you get past this fence?" Blondie probed. "Sure 'nough, little lady," I beamed. "There's not a fence, I can't get over, under, or around. Well, not many fences, anyhow. Let me have a look and see."

I reared up and put my front feet on the gate, and pushed hard. Sure'nough, Ralph had left a little slack 'tween the gate and the fence post. I pushed my head 'tween the gate and fence post. It took some huffin' and puffin', but I finally got through. "My hero," Blondie glowed. "Shucks, that's nothin'," I bragged. "Now, let me see if there's any fresh hay for you to lie on." I looked the pen over, and found some hay scattered 'bout, so I raked it into a shady corner, with my nose. It took a few minutes, and I got a little dirt up my nose, yuck, but it were worth it! Blondie looked so pleased. It was a pleasure to help her! "There, that oughta be comfy," I affirmed. "Are you hungry?" "Yes, I haven't eaten since yesterday."

Blondie purred. "Well, Ralph put a little grain in the trough over yonder," I pointed out. "Let me look 'round to see if there is somethin' else sanitary, that you can eat." "General, can I go with you?" Billy asked. "Negative," I snapped. "This here's a job for the head of the Sanitation Department, know what I mean?" "But I'm, good at gathering up straw and such. Please let me come, please!" "No, Billy, I ordered.

"Besides, your gate is hard to open with the latch bein' off the ground, so high and all. No, this is a job for the General." I slipped through the gate and just had to do a little dance, before I left to find some sanitary food for Blondie. First, I reared up on my hind feet, then I boxed the air with my front two paws. Next, I jumped into the air a couple of times, with my head bent almost to my stomach. Finally, for good measure, I laid down and rolled over three or four times. I was so happy! Blondie is the best thing that ever happened on this here ranch, know what I mean?

I searched for a long time, 'cause I wanted to find the best sanitary food for Blondie. Gramma Grass just wouldn't do and neither would Johnson Grass. That is mostly what the ranch had, though. Then it hit me like a ton of bricks. Sunflowers! Sunflowers are sweet to the taste, and they look good, too. Seemed like I had to walk over half the ranch to find a bunch of Sunflowers. I chewed 'em off close to the ground, then I picked 'em up in my teeth, and carried 'em back to the barn.

When I got there, I found Billy playing his favorite game. "Blondie, did you ever look at the moon?" "Why yes, it's very beautiful when it is round and full. Why do you ask?" "Rachel once told me a story about the moon being made out of green cheese. Is that true?" Billy asked. 'Billy,' I yelled, "I told ya that Blondie has had a hard day and doesn't need all your ignorant questions." "But what about the moon?" Billy protested. "It's ok, General dear," Blondie affirmed.

"Billy, that's a fairy tale. If the moon were green cheese, it would melt when the sun came out. Understand?" "Yes, thank you," Billy replied. "Now, General, what did you bring me?" "Sunflowers," I beamed. "I had to walk the ranch over to find 'em." "I just love sunflowers, thank you," Blondie sighed. "Wanna share them with me?", I asked. "Sure 'nough," said Blondie. Them sunflowers is how me and Blondie got engaged. Private had his head stuck in the pigpen, the whole time.

CHAPTER 6

Jack Junior

I had one of the best nights of my life, me and Blondie curled up together on the hay in the corner of the barn. After we ate the Sunflowers, we shared some pleasant conversation. We talked late into the night. It was heaven on earth. I think I'm in love... Also, we think Jack Junior is on the way!

Next mornin', I was woke up in the rudest manner. Ralph grabbed me by the horns, and dragged me out of Blondie's pen. I didn't go easy, know what I mean? I pulled, tugged, and reared up, but it didn't do no good. Ralph was too strong. He threw me out of Blondie's pen, and shut the gate. He then fixed the latch on the gate so that I couldn't squeeze through.

Rachel took pity on me. She knew I was broken hearted because Ralph had separated me from my lady. She petted my back, and scratched behind my ears. Man, nothin' beats a good ear scratchin', know what I mean? She talked to me quietly, while Ralph did his chores. After that, they left in Ralph's chariot. "General, why does Ralph keep separatin' you from Blondie?" Billy questioned. "Ain't it as obvious as the nose on your face?" I answered. "Well, no" Billy confessed. "Is it because he wants you to do your sanitation work, while Blondie and Gomez keep me company?" Billy reasoned. "No, you mule headed idiot," I snorted.

"It's because Ralph wants Blondie and Gomez to mate." "Oh my," Blondie gasped. "That's 'k by meee," Gomez chimed in, still eatin' pig food. "That's 'nough, Private," I ordered. We don't need any more of that kinda talk, understand?" "But why does Ralph want Blondie and Gomez to mate?" Billy continued to question. "I reckon it's because they're both Spanish goats." I answered. "But the fact of the matter is, that me and Blondie are done married, know what I mean? I aims to get in that pen, just as soon as I make my rounds. Private, you look after things while I'm gone, understand?" "Se" Gomez answered, as he munched happily away. By goin' off alone, I broke one of my safety rules. I always insisted that we goats go into the pasture in groups of two or more. It was dangerous, because of coyotes. There were two especially worrisome coyotes, named Booger and Digger. They's sneak up on you, before you could wink and eye. I don't rightly know how they done it. Coyotes are just sneaky. One lucky thing though, they are dumb as dirt.

Anywho, I hadn't seen Booger and Digger for a while, so I went about my business. I found some tasty tin cans that Ralph had left in the dump. Boy, were they good. I ate the paper labels, and all, yum!

Directly, I heard this noise. It sounded like breathin'. No, two somebodies were breathin'. I looked 'round, and there was Booger and Digger, not ten feet away. "Looks like we're gonna have lamb chops tonight," Digger sneered. "Goat, you dumb dumb," Booger corrected. "We're gonna have goat chops for supper." "Hi guys," I replied casually. "Haven't seen you 'round much." "We're back," Booger replied, with a snarl. "That's right, Bonehead," Digger joined in.

"We've returned to reclaim our territory." "Your territory..." I interjected, then I stopped because only a fool gets into an argument with a coyote. "Yes, this is our territory, but right now, we have supper on our minds," Digger said. "Oh, you two looking for some rabbit stew?" I questioned. Rabbit is a coyote's favorite meal. "Rabbit?", Booger asked, almost drooling. "Sure 'nough," I encouraged. "There's a momma rabbit and a nest of babies in that old hot water heater over..." I didn't even get to finish my sentence, before Booger and Digger took off in search of a mythical rabbit dinner. I took my leave, and headed for the barn. Coyotes don't liked to be tricked.

CHAPTER 7

Pa

Finally, the time arrived for Jack Junior to be born. Wow! I am one proud Dad! He is a dandy! Well, excuse me. Where are my manners? I've introduced you to Blondie, Gomez, Jack Junior, myself, and you've met Billy, too, but there are lots of other interesting animals on this here ranch.

One of the most interesting critters is named, "Pa," because he's the daddy of most of the cattle 'round here. There's more cattle on the ranch, than any other critters. Pa's big, I mean really big. I have to crane my neck to see his eyes. His face is white, and the rest of him is red, except for two feet, which have white socks, and the tip of his tail is white, too. Pa has got horns. I used to think that my horns were somethin' special, until I met Pa. His horns are massive, and they turn up, instead of layin' back on the head, like my horns do. Pa drinks from the water trough alone, because his head and horns take up all the room! A body don't wanna mess with them horns, know what I mean? Did I mention that Pa is tall? He's taller than Ralph. The top of Ralph's head just barely reaches Pa's ears. He's a little shorter than Billy, but he's much broader and stronger. He can push any of the cows out of the way, if they try to get his food. None of the cattle mess with Pa. He stands alone, know what I mean?

I once saw Pa get in a fight with a pack of coyotes. Booger and Digger, and a couple of their buddies, surrounded a calf named Jamie, and were about to have "baby Beef Wellington," for lunch. Pa came to her rescue, just in time. He lifted Booger six feet off the ground with his horns, and kicked Digger into the next county. The rest ran off. Digger disappeared for a while. I don't want you thinkin' I'm afraid of Pa. No sir! I ain't afraid of nothin'. Respect is the word I prefer. I has a deep respect for Pa... Even though there are dozens of cattle on the ranch, I hardly ever see them. They graze on the far side of the ranch, and they water in the larger pond. Pa isn't much of a talker, either. Why just the other day, I saw him at the pond, and tried to carry on a friendly conversation. "Hello, Pa," I said. 'How's everythin' goin'?" "Hummm," he said. Then he just turned 'round and walked off. How in the world is a feller supposed to have a conversation, if he's the only one talkin?

Boo and Toot make up for Pa's lack of conversation skills. They are two of the friendlier cows on the ranch. Boo got her name, because she's afraid of everything. Toot, well, let's just say that some unpleasant odors come from her direction, from time to time. When Pa ended our conversation by walking off, they took over. "Don't mind Pa, Jack, he's the strong and silent, type," Boo said. "I've had better conversations with a fence post," Toot added. "That's right," Boo inserted. "He rarely speaks to any of us cows, unless there is some kind of danger, or it's mating season." "He's a real charmer, when it's mating season," Toot said. (psssssst) "Not again, Toot!" Boo exclaimed. "Can't you turn that thing off, for even a few minutes?" "Oh my gosh, Toot," I roared. "You smell worse than the pigs. Stand over there." "Sorry, I'll try to be more careful. Like I was saying, Pa can be real charming during mating season. He can also carry on a good conversation, if he has a mind to." He can make a girl's heart melt...ohhh, what's that?" Boo asked, in a trembling voice. "Relax, Honey," Toot admonished. "It's only Jamie bumping your utters, so she can nurse." "Oh, thank goodness," responded Boo. I thought a coyote might have snuck up on me. "Well, ladies, it was good to see ya," I interrupted. "But I've gotta get along. Tell Pa hello for me." "Bye -Bye for now," Toot called out. "Tell Blondie and Junior hello, for me," Boo added.

Yes, Boo and Toot, are quite the pair. Unlike Pa, they don't hardly know when to stop talkin'. Thank goodness, the other cattle aren't so friendly. I'd hardly get any sanitation work done, if I had to talk to all them cattle, as much as I do to Boo and Toot.

Two other critters on the ranch aren't as interestin' as Pa and the rest of the cattle. Chop and Porky are two pigs. They have a pen near our water trough. They both have round heads, and long round snouts. They have short legs, and a curly tail. They are pink all over, 'cept for their eyes. Noisy, there's nothin' worse than a squealin' pig. All they do is eat and sleep. It's like I said, pigs is about as interesting, as dirt. Every now and again, I have to keep them in line, and remind them who's boss. One day Porky griped at Gomez, because he was eatin' the pig food. "You had better stop eating our food, Gomez." Porky ordered. "That's right, goat boy," Chop added. "There's barely'nough food for me, so keep your dumb goat head out of our pen, or you just might get one of your ears bit off." I was takin' a nap, and might of missed the whole thing, but Gomez started cryin'. When I arrived at the pigs' feed trough, Gomez had his head stuck in the fence, and Chop had his self a mouth full of goat ear. "That's 'nough of that," I shouted at Chop. "It's Jack," Porky whispered to Chop. "That's right, pig head. You two better take a nap, and leave Gomez, alone. If one tiny piece of his ear is missin', I'm coming over this fence, and knock some sense into the both of ya" "Ok, Jack," Chop gulped. " I'm kind of tired anyhow. Come on Porky. It's nap time."

Them pigs think they is mean, but they're just plain yellow. They run from more trouble, than any other critter I know.

Another thing about pigs, they smell. Yuck! They poop and pee on the ground, then roll in it. Boy that's kinda dumb, know what I mean? Even Toot's gas can't compare to a pig's smell, 'nough said. One last thing about hogs, they just love to root 'round. They find a spot of soft ground, or a muddy place, and the next thing you know, they's rootin'. They stick their nose to the ground and push. I've seen them root up grass and Sunflowers, and all kinds of other plants.

I'll never forget one time I was nappin', and Chop was rootin' 'round the pig pen. He had turned up a lot of dirt, when suddenly, he let out one of them ear piercin' squeals of his. Seems that as he was rootin', he ran into a pipe, buried in the ground. Well, I couldn't sleep no more, what, with all that dad blamed noise. I got up, and went to have a look at Chop. When I got to the fence, his nose was bleedin'. I guess he cut his self on the buried pipe. Man oh man, I got some good laughs outta that one. Well, there you have it. I've introduced you to the main critters, on the ranch. Sure, there are other wild critters, like birds, snakes, and skunks, but they don't come 'round the barn much. All in all, it's a good life here on the farm. I just love bein' Head of the Sanitation Department.

One afternoon, not too long ago, me and Gomez was having a good long nap. I was dreamin' about finding some delicious sanitary stuff, on the back side of the ranch. All of a sudden, I was woke up by all this noise. I opened one eye to take a peep, then I jumped up quick as a flash. Ralph was driving up in his horseless chariot. Follow'n him was another horseless chariot, and even another one. The second one was bigger than Ralph's, and it made an awful noise. Why, it almost broke my eardrums, listen'n to it.

Anywho, both chariots pulled up to the barn. Ralph got outta his chariot first. When the other feller got outta his chariot, I knowed that we was in deep trouble. I'd seen this feller before. Ralph called him, "The Vet." Whenever he shows up, some goat gets hurt. Last time he was here, he trimmed my horns, by cuttin' the tips off with a thing-o-ma-jig, that looked like a pair of big scissors. The dang fool cut off too much of my horn, and made it bleed. I must have bled a gallon or two. I bet that there was 'nough blood to paint the barn.... Well, almost 'nough. Hurt, a body never felt such pain! Oh my, makes me shiver, just to think 'bout it.

This time, the vet didn't have no scissors with him. Thank goodness! That's a relief! Instead, he had this big straw with him. The straw was about two feet long, and as big'round as a cat's tail. Ralph and the Vet headed for Billy first. The Vet lifted up one of Billy's front legs. He looked at his horseshoe, and cleaned out all the gunk inside it. He then checked all four legs out, just a lift'n and cleanin'. Then, the Vet looked in both of Billy's ears. After that, he opened his mouth, and checked his teeth. When he finished the exam, he reached into this shirt pocket, and pulled out this huge pill. That dad blamed pill was as big as a quarter. Quick as a flash, he put that pill into the big straw. He then put one end of the straw in Billy's mough, and his mouth on the other end, so he could blow the pill into Billy's mouth. What happened next, can only be described as "funny", just hilarious. As I said, the Vet put the pill in the straw, then one end of the straw into Billy's mouth, and the other end in his own mouth. When the Vet took a deep breath, well sir, all I can say is that Billy blowed first. The Vet stood straight up and swallowed that pill. His face turned red as a beet, and he started cough'n and jump'n up and down, on one foot, and then the other. I never laughed so hard in my life. Know what I mean?

They then went for Junior, but had a hard time catchin' him. They got him cornered a time or two, but he got away. Then Ralph jumped at Junior a time or two. He fell flat on his face, and the ground kinda shook, know what I mean? Finally, Ralph grabbed on to one of Junior's hind legs. That's all it took, Junior was caught. First thing they did, was to take hold of one of his ears. The Vet pulled out a long thin knife, and poked a hole in Junior's ear. Man that's gotta hurt. It made his ear bleed, too. They then put this big yellow tag in his ear. That tag looked plumb silly, just a hang'n in his ear, know what I mean?

Next, Ralph and the Vet gives Blondie the eyeball. That's when I lost it. No one's gonna touch my woman. So, I lowered my head and ran as fast as I could, straight at the Vet. Caught him right in the buttox. Well sir, the Vet fell forward, and stabbed Ralph with the big needle. Ralph started yelling, and hopping on one foot, then the other. You would have thought that he hit his finger with a hammer, the way he carried on. He acted just like a big baby. Best thing of all, the needle got bent giv'n Ralph a shot, so the Vet weren't able to give no more shots that day. That's a good thing, know what I mean?

The Vet picked up his big straw, and climbed into this chariot. Ralph got into his chariot, too. They both drove off. Good riddance, is all I can say. "Blondie, are you ok?" I asked. "Yes, Jack, thank you for saving me from that awful needle. I'm mighty grateful. Later on, I'll show my appreciation to you." Whoa, you could have knocked me over with a feather. Boy, I can't wait till tonight. Meantime, me and Gomez went out to the back side of the ranch, to sees if we could find anything sanitary to eat.

CHAPTER 9

Danger

Yes sir, life here on the ranch, is good! I's just loves my job as head of the Sanitation Department. The only bad thing on the ranch is the summer. The weather, it sure do get hot. The only thing a body can do to cool off, is to get a long slow drink from the water trough, and lay down in the corner of the barn, so that you're out of the sunlight.

The pigs have it the best on them hot days, cause Ralph sprays water on the ground with a hose. Some of the water soaks into the ground and makes mud. Them pigs likes to lay in the mud, and get their belly coated with it. They rolls over, and gets that slimy gunk all over their back. Next thing you knows, they go to rootin' in the mud, and that gunk gets all over their snout and ears. What a mess! I guess it keeps them cool though, 'cause they rolls in the mud every chance they get.

One hot summer day, me, Blondie, and Junior got a long cool drink from the water trough, then took a long nap on a soft place in the hay. I was tired and sleepin' hard, when all of a sudden, I hears Pork give a loud squeal, followed by a "Watchout, Junior!" Quick as a flash, me and Blondie was awake. Junior was over at the pig pen, with his head through the slats in the fence, just chow'n down on the pig's food. Then I heard it, the unmistakable rattle of a snake. Sure 'nough, there was a big rattler, coiled up next to the pig's feed trough. I guess he was shadein' his self from the hot sun. Anyhow, when Junior got too close to him, he shook his tail, and was ready to strike. Poor Junior had learned that the rattle he heard, meant danger. I knowed of one goat, that got himself bit on the nose by one of them rattlers. He swelled up so much, that it looked like he had two noses. Next day the poor critter died. He couldn't drink or eat nothin'. Wow, what a terrible way to go!

Anyhow, Junior's eatin' out of the pig's trough, and this big rattler is all coiled up and ready to strike. Me and Blondie gets up real fast and heads to the pig's trough, so we can help Junior. Quicker than greased lightnin', Pork jumped up from his mud puddle, and heads for the feed trough. When he was a couple of feet from that rattler, he rares up on his hind legs and brings his front paws down on that snake's head. The snake straightens his self out, stiff as a board. Pork rares up again, and bangs that rattler on the head a second time. After that, Pork picks the snake up by it's tail, and throws it over to Chop. By this time, Chop is out of the mud puddle, and he starts bangin'on the snake's head, with his paws. After stompin on the varmint several times, Chop grabs hold of its tail, and gives it a fling. That snake flew head over tail, about twenty feet and landed outside the pigpen. He didn't move no more, so I think he was dead.

When Blondie and I reached Junior, we looked him over, and saw that he was ok. Then, we let out a big sigh of relief. As soon as Junior realized that he could've been bit by that rattler and died, he started crying. Blondie took him to get a drink of water. I stood quietly by the pigs, for a minute. I weren't sure what to say, besides that I had me a lump in my throat, that made it hard for a feller to swaller, or to say anything. Finally, I managed to croak out the words, "Thanks boys." Then I went over to check on Blondie and Junior.

CHAPTER 10

Rachel's Outing

On another hot day, me and the family was layin' on some cool hay. I'd just dozed off, and was dreamin' of finding some sanitary food on the far side of the ranch. All of a sudden, I was woke up by the rattlin' of Ralph's truck After he stopped that worn out bucket of bolts, he gets out, and starts fixin' some fence over by Billy's pen. Rachel was with him, and when she got out of the truck, I noticed that she had on her gettin' wet clothes. I think she called them "a swimsuit." She was carryin' the prettiest red towel, that a body ever saw. I gets up and follows her to the pond. Gomez came along, too, but Blondie and Junior stayed at the barn, to get some more z's.

When we got to the pond, Rachel found herself a small styrofoam raft. It weren't more than a couple of feet wide, and maybe twice that long. Anyhow, she pushed the raft a couple of feet away from the shore, and then climbed on. She used her hands to paddle out to the middle of the pond. Directly, she Iayed herself down on the raft, and was soon fast asleep. Me and Gomez laid down on the grassy shore, and took ourselves a nap. Next thing I know, I hears Rachel yellin' my name. I jumps up quick like, and sees that Rachel had fallen off the raft, and was drownin'! I guess that she couldn't swim none, know what I mean? I ordered the Private, to go to the barn, and find Ralph. Meanwhile, I jumps into the lake, and swims out to Rachel. She grabbed onto my collar, and I swam back to the shore with her. It sure was a long swim, and I got plenty worn out, but we made it! When we were safely on shore, I fell down, panting something fierce. Rachel and I laid there a long time... Directly, Ralph drives up in his truck. Rachel told him how she fell off the raft, and how I saved her from drownin'. Ralph picked her up and carried her to his truck, and they drove back to the barn. Me and Gomez followed along kinda slow like. When we got back to the barn, Rachel had filled our water trough with fresh cool water. She also filled our feed trough with a double sized portion of grain. Wow, what a great reward!

Well sir, I dived right into that feed trough, and stuffed my face full of that ole grain. Gomez was standin'a few feet away, and not eatin' nothin. That was ok by me, cause it meant that there was more for me to eat. Rachel started scratchin' behind my ears. Man oh man, that felt good! Next thing I knowed, Gomez started coughin'. His coughin' got louder and louder. Rachel went over to see what was wrong with him. There was somethin' red stickin'out of his mouth. She grabbed a hold of it and started pulling. It took her several tugs, but she finally pulled that red towel out of Gomez's mouth. That towel weren't so pretty no more, know what I mean?...

CHAPTER 11

Wrestling with Coyotes

Early one morning, me, Blondie, Junior, and Gomez got busy with our sanitation job. By noon, we worked ourselves to the far side of the ranch. found all kinds of sanitary food. We even found two or three bunches of sunflowers. I let Junior and Blondie have them, 'cause that's what a gentleman does, know what I mean?

By late afternoon, we'd almost gotten to the barn. It had been a wonderful day, filled with family and lots of good food. Anywho, we was a grazin', when I hears breathin'. I looked up and spotted a pack of coyotes stalking Junior. Booger and Digger were leading the way. Quick as a flash, one of them varmints grabbed Junior by the neck, and flung him to the ground. Booger was just about to clamp down on Junior's neck, when I arrived on the scene. "You'd better back off Goat Boy," Booger snarled, " 'Cause there's five of us, and only one of you." "Don't let that bother you none," I said. "One goat can take care of five coyotes every day of the week, and twice on Sunday." With that I lowered my head, and charged at Booger. My horns caught him in the ribs, and knocked him down. Two of the other coyotes grabbed a hold of me, one on each side of my neck! I turned my head hard to the right side, and throwed off one of them coyotes. He rolled three times across that grass, before he came to a stop. Then, I jerked my neck away from the other coyote. That's when I called for Gomez to help me, but that dad blame fool, was playing dead. He heard another goat say, that he fell down and played dead, when another goat was attacked by coyotes, and the coyotes left him alone. I knowed better, though. I knowed that if a goat played dead, that them coyotes would have him for lunch. That's why I fought so hard, and why I yelled for Blondie to get Billy. She and Junior took off like a flash.

I lowered my head and charged at the coyote, which was next to me. I caught his hind side with my horns, and lifted him off the ground. Then, I throwed him off to one side. After that, some of them coyotes made a big circle around me. One of them nipped my right ear, while another one bit the lower part of my left hind leg. Then, they all jumped on me at once. One coyote bit into the top of my neck, while another one sank his teeth into my belly. Next thing I knowed, I was on the ground with all the coyotes standin' over me.

That's when I felt the ground shakin', and I heard donkey hooves poundin' the ground, hard like. I knowed that Billy was comin'. He put his big nose under the belly of one of them coyotes, and picked him up, four feet off the ground, and flung the varmint about fifteen feet away. Then, Billy started kicking those coyotes with his hind legs. When he kicked Booger's jaw, I heard a loud crunch. I bet that kick broke his jaw, know what I mean?

Well sir, it didn't take them coyotes long to realize that they was out classed. They disappeared, just as quickly as they had appeared. I was layed out on the ground, panting hard. My life had flashed before my eyes that day, know what I mean?

Next thing I knowed, Blondie was standing over me asking if I was ok. I got to my feet, and nearly fell back to the ground. Blondie stood beside me, to kinda steady me. Boy, what a day! Very slowly, we all walked back to the barn, and I collapsed on some soft hay. Junior laid on my right side, and Blondie was on my left. We was like three peas in a pod.

That's when I noticed that Billy was standing over us. "Billy," I asked, "Why aren't you in your pen?" "Well, sir," he said, "The gate won't latch no more, so I thought I'd stand over here, and visit with you folks." "Why won't the gate latch?", I asked. "Because it broke when I kicked it open to come help you."

"Oh yeah, well thanks again," I said. "Billy, you deserves a reward for what you done for me. You can ask Blondie all the questions you want." After the one hundredth question, I fell fast asleep.

Another big thing here on the ranch, is the "Stock Show." Every year, Ralph and Rachel works us goats into shape, for the "Stock Show." Part of gettin' in shape, is walking. Just the other day, Rachel came to the barn with a leash. A leash means one thing to a goat, it's time for a walk. Anywho, she puts the leash on Gomez's collar. When she started walkin', Gomez ran off the other way. He took off so fast, that he jerked Rachel off her feet, and partly into the water trough. She rolled to the ground. Her right arm and shoulder were soaked. She even got some water on her stomach and chest. It was a cold day, and Rachel went to shiverin' something fierce. Ralph saw what happened, and came a runnin'. He picked Rachel up off the ground, then took the leash off of Gomez. After that, he and Rachel drove off in his rattle trap of a truck. The walk was over for that day.

The next day, Ralph and Rachel returned for another walk. This time, Ralph decided to help Rachel walk Gomez. Ralph hooked Gomez to the leash. Mostly, Ralph had to pull Gomez along, 'cause that dumb goat didn't want to walk none. Anywho, they walked out of the pens, with Ralph a pullin' and Gomez just stumblin' along. They hadn't gone very far, when Gomez sped up, and walked in front of Ralph. He tripped over Gomez, and fell hard on the ground. Ralph's fall made the ground shake, know what I mean? Ralph sat up and pulled Gomez close to him. Then, he doubled up his fist, and hit Gomez hard on his nose. Bet that hurt! Rachel scolded Ralph for hitting Gomez. Ralph replied that "Gomez was the dumbest goat that he's ever met." I couldn't agree more. When the good Lord was givin' out brains to goats, Gomez thought the Lord said, "Trains." Gomez went in the opposite direction.

Ralph tried to walk Gomez one more time. He hooked the leash onto Gomez's collar, then he half dragged, and half-pulled Gomez out of the barn, and into the open field. Ralph tied one end of the leash to the bumper of his truck, then he and Rachel jumped inside the truck, and took off real slow. Gomez took two or three steps, and then the fool laid down. Can you believe it? He just laid down, and Ralph drug him for ten or fifteen feet. Ralph took off real slow a second time, and Gomez did the same thing. He walked a few steps, and then fell down, again. Ralph tried a third time, with the same results. Finally, Ralph wised up, and let Gomez off the leash! The next time that he and Rachel came to walk the goat, they hooked me to the leash, and we had us a fine walk.

A few days later, Ralph and Rachel drove up, and he was pullin' a cattle trailer behind his truck. The gate on the trailer was built to slide side to side, rather than swing out. This allowed the trailer to get real close to our pen. Once the trailer was parked, Ralph and Rachel got out and ambled into the barn. They came right up to me, and hooked the leash to my collar. They led me into the trailer, and tied my leash to a hook, inside. Rachel sat down beside me, and rubbed my ears. Man, I sure do like it when she does that. Meanwhile, Ralph got out of the trailer, and shut it's gate. He then got into his rattle trap of a truck, and started it up. Before I knowed it, we were at the pens by the "Stock Show." Ralph parked near a small wooden building, and opened the gate on the trailer. Me and Rachel stepped out. Inside the building, there was a wash bay for goats. Rachel and I walked into the bay, and she took off my leash and collar. Next, she picked up a water hose, and sprayed warm water all over me. She then squirted a little dish soap on my back, and started rubbing me down. She rubbed my back and shoulders. She even washed my underneath side. Man that warm water sure felt good, on such a cold day.

After my bath, Rachel dried me off with that fluffy red towel of hers. She started with my head, and dried behind my ears. Then, she dried my shoulders and back. Man, I never felt so good in my whole life.

She finished, by drying my belly and legs. That was followed by a good brushing. A fellow never looked as good as I did, after my washin', dryin', and brushin'. Followin' that, we went into a small pen, where I got a haircut. One of the fellers there had a pair of electric clippers that sounded like a swarm of bumblebees a buzzin'. Anyhow, he started with my left shoulder, and worked his way to my hip. He clipped upwards toward my back, and over to my right shoulder, with those clippers just buzzin' away. He clipped all over my body, except for my head and the tip of my tail. The end of my tail looked like a huge pom pom. Have you ever heard of such a silly thing?

Later on, Rachel put me in a small pen, and gave me some fresh water and feed. That water went down smooth, cause I'd worked up a big time thirst, gettin' ready for the "Stock Show."

In the pen next to me, was two sheep. They was both white a-11 over, except for their black nose and eyes. When one of those sheep turned it's head to the right, the other one did too. When one of them said hello to me, the other one did too. That's the dumbest thing I've ever seen. As a result, I named them "Dumb" and "Dumber." I ignored them, and turned my back side to 'em, while I cleaned up my feed trough.

Next morning, Rachel woke me real early. She brushed me down one more time, then hooked the leash on me. Before I knowed it, we was standin' in line, and waitin' our turn to go into the show arena. There was three other goats standin' in line with us. They was our competition, for the big "Stock Show." There was one other African Goat, like me. The other ones, was those scrawny Spanish Goats. Before I knowed what was goin' on, we was in the big arena. Rachel walked me slowly around the arena, while this one dude looked us over. At one point, Rachel stopped walking, and the feller looked real close at me. He looked inside my ears, and even pryed open my mouth, and looked inside. He done the same thing, with the other three goats. Then, the feller wrote down some stuff on his clipboard. After that, this pretty young girl, handed out ribbons to each one of the children. They gave Rachel a red one. It was a lot more pretty, than the blue, white, and yellow ribbons, that she gave the other kids. I guess that means that I was the best of the bunch. Shucks, I could have told you that, before the "Stock Show" started.

CHAPTER 13

The Cow Dog

I almost forgot to tell you about one critter here on the ranch. His name is George, and he's a cow dog. He used to come to the barn with Ralph and Rachel, but not so much lately. That's ok by me, cause I don't like him none, cause he's an arrogant know it all. He has short blue hair, and a stub of a tail. His nose and eyes are black. I beat him up one day, so he don't come here much, now.

I remember the day I beat him up, like it were yesterday. I was nappin' on the hay in the barn, while Junior and Blondie were grazin' in a field close by. I was rudely woke up, when Ralph drove up in his horseless carriage. Rachel wasn't with him that day. He brung George, instead. George hopped out of the truck, and started sniffin' 'round. That dog sniffs everythin'. Most things he sniffs, he marks, by lifting his hind leg, and peein' on it.

When he walked by me, he hurled an insult, "Hello there, Dummy." Can you believe it? He actually called me "Dummy." Why, I'm the smartest critter in the barn. I'm even the smartest critter on the ranch. I let his off color remark pass, cause I was tired. Besides all of that, it was too hot to get into a ruckus with George.

George continued his journey 'round the barn, marking the water trough, and feed bin. I closed my eyes, to resume my nap, as he left the barn, and into one of the nearby fields.

A littte bit later, I heard Blondie yelling at George. She said, "leave me a-lone, you brute." Then I heard her scream in pain, and call out my name. "Jack, come quick." I was awake and bright eyed, in a flash. My woman called for me, and I came a runnin'. What I saw when I got outside the barn, made my blood boil I was mad enough to spit nails, cause I saw George chasin' Blondie 'round in a circle, and bitin' her tail.

I lowered my head, and charged toward George, as fast as my legs would carry me. I caught him broadside along his rib cage, and knocked him off his feet. Quick as a flash, George was back on his feet. He was growlin' and showin' his teeth. Yes sir, George was lookin' for a fight, and I was just the feller to give it to him. I turned 'round and gave him a swift kick in the mouth. He let out a loud yelp, and ran off and hid under Ralph's truck. Fight over, Jack won, and George lost.

Another time when George came for a visit, he darned near got himself killed,by one of them rattlesnakes. George was snifflin' 'round the feed barrel, when he found the critter. Guess the snake was waitin' on a rat, to get a snack from one of our feed sacks. Anyhow, George was sniffin' 'round, when he came by the rattler. The dang fool tried to sniff it. The snake went to rattlin' his tail, and he struck at George two or three times, but never did hit the mark. I was layin' on a bed of soft hay on the other side of the barn, and saw the whole thing.

Anywho, George started barkin' and tryin' to bite the snake's neck. The snake kept rattlin' and strikin' at George. It was quite a show! Suddenly, Ralph shows up to see what George was barkin' at. He grabbed a hoe, which hung on the wall of the barn, and whacked the snake a time or two. The snake stopped rattlin', and rolled over on it's back, with it's yellow belly facing up for everyone to see.

When Ralph was sure that the snake was dead, he pulled his knife out of his pocket, and opened the biggest blade. He then cut the snake's head off, and the rattlers, too. There must have been ten or twelve buttons, on that horrid snake's tail.

Printed in the United States
by Baker & Taylor Publisher Services